Plant Parts

Flowers

Revised Edition

by Vijaya Khisty Bodach
Consulting Editor: Gail Saunders-Smith, PhD

Consultant: Judson R. Scott, Former President
American Society of Consulting Arborists

CAPSTONE PRESS
a capstone imprint

Pebble Plus is published by Capstone Press,
1710 Roe Crest Drive, North Mankato, Minnesota 56003.
www.mycapstone.com

Copyright © 2007, 2016 by Capstone Press, a Capstone imprint. All rights reserved.

No part of this publication may be reproduced in whole or in part, or stored in a retrieval system, or transmitted in any form or by any means, electronic, mechanical, photocopying, recording, or otherwise, without written permission of the publisher. For information regarding permission, write to Capstone Press, 1710 Roe Crest Drive, North Mankato, Minnesota 56003.

Library of Congress Cataloging-in-Publication Data is available on the Library of Congress website.

ISBN: 978-1-5157-4243-2 (revised paperback)
ISBN: 978-1-5157-4352-1 (ebook pdf)

Editorial Credits
Sarah L. Schuette, editor; Jennifer Bergstrom, designer; Kelly Garvin, photo researcher/photo editor

Photo Credits
Capstone Studio: Karon Dubke, cover; Shutterstock: Aleksey Stemmer, (sun flowers) 22, Angel DiBilio, 13, Anna Moskvina, 11, Balakirev Vladimir, 1, Bildagentur Zoonar GmbH, 7, Bogdan Wankowicz, (seed) 22, janaph, 19, Olga Prolygina, 15, SusaZoom, 21, Thanamat Somwan, 17, vandame, 5, Varina Patel, 9

Note to Parents and Teachers

The Plant Parts set supports national science standards related to identifying plant parts and the diversity and interdependence of life. This book describes and illustrates flowers. The images support early readers in understanding the text. The repetition of words and phrases helps early readers learn new words. This book also introduces early readers to subject-specific vocabulary words, which are defined in the Glossary section. Early readers may need assistance to read some words and to use the Table of Contents, Glossary, Read More, Internet Sites, and Index sections of the book.

Table of Contents

Plants Need Flowers 4
All Kinds of Flowers 12
Flowers We Eat. 16
Wonderful Flowers. 20

Parts of a Sunflower 22
Glossary 23
Read More 23
Index 24
Internet Sites. 24

Plants Need Flowers

Flowers make seeds
and fruits for plants.
Flowers come in many colors,
shapes, and sizes.

Flower buds grow
from the stem of a plant.
The buds open
and flowers bloom.

Flowers have pollen inside.
Pollen helps flowers
make seeds.

Parts of the flower

turn into fruit.

Seeds grow inside the fruit.

New plants grow from seeds.

All Kinds of Flowers

Colorful flower petals attract birds. The birds sip on nectar inside the flowers.

Roses have soft petals that smell good.

Roses grow on bushes.

Flowers We Eat

We eat some flowers.

Cauliflower is a white flower.

We eat it raw or cooked.

Artichokes are flower buds.
They make good dips
and sauces.

Wonderful Flowers

Pretty or plain,

large or small,

flowers help plants

make fruit and seeds.

Parts of a Sunflower

flower

seed

root

stem

leaves

Glossary

attract—to be interested or drawn closer to something

bud—a small shoot on a plant that grows into a flower or a leaf; buds grow from plant stems.

nectar—the sweet liquid inside flowers

pollen—tiny yellow grains made in flowers

seed—the part of a flowering plant that can grow into a new plant

stem—the long main part of a plant that makes leaves

Read More

Blackaby, Susan. *Buds and Blossoms: A Book About Flowers.* Growing Things. Minneapolis: Picture Window Books, 2003.

Branigan, Carrie, and Richard Dunne. *Flowers and Seeds.* World of Plants. North Mankato, Minn.: Smart Apple Media, 2005.

Schaefer, Lola M. *Pick, Pull, Snap!: Where Once a Flower Bloomed.* New York: Greenwillow Books, 2003.

Index

artichokes, 18

bloom, 6

buds, 6, 18

cauliflower, 16

fruits, 4, 10, 20

nectar, 12

petals, 12, 14

pollen, 8

roses, 14

seeds, 4, 8, 10, 20

stem, 6

Word Count: 118
Grade: 1
Early-Intervention Level: 15

Internet Sites

FactHound offers a safe, fun way to find Internet sites related to this book. All of the sites on FactHound have been researched by our staff.

Here's how:

1. Visit www.facthound.com

2. Choose your grade level.

3. Type in this book ID **0736863427** for age-appropriate sites. You may also browse subjects by clicking on letters, or by clicking on pictures and words.

4. Click on the **Fetch It** button.

Facthound will fetch the best sites for you!